There's a Fly in my Swill

Brant Parker and Johnny Hart

CORONET BOOKS
Hodder Fawcett, London

First Published by Fawcett Publications Inc.,
New York 1973

Copyright © 1967, 1968 by
Publishers Newspaper Syndicate,
Copyright © 1973 by Fawcett Publications, Inc.

Published by special arrangement with
Publishers-Hall Syndicate, Inc.

Coronet edition 1974
Fourth impression 1981

Printed and bound in Great Britain for
Coronet Books, Hodder Fawcett, London,
by Hunt Barnard Printing Ltd,
Aylesbury, Bucks.

ISBN 0 340 18604 6

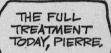

CREAKK

N
A
B!

4-25

IS BLANCH SWIMMING TODAY?

NO... SHE'S OUT SHOPPING.

9-28

THERE'S A WHALE IN THE MOAT!

Publishers-Hall Syndicate, 1967 E. Parker

10-14

10-19

10-25

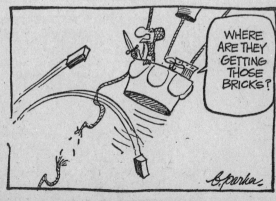

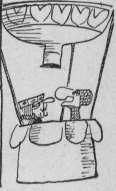

3

4

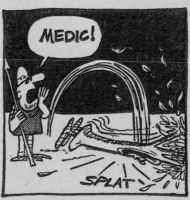

12-23

12-27

5

1-11

YAAAGHH!

GNAW
GNAW
CHOMP
GNASH
SLURP

SWOOSH

1-30

I ALWAYS **WONDERED** WHY THEY STUCK A NAPKIN UNDER THEIR CHIN.

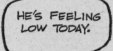

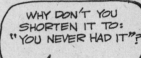

SIRE, WHY DO YOU LET THOSE GOOD-FOR-NOTHING HIPPIES HANG AROUND?

3-11

WHAT DO YOU MEAN, GOOD-FOR-NOTHING?...

...THEY KEEP THE RATS OUT OF THE ABANDONED TENEMENTS.

3-19

3-23

4-3